THE TWINS

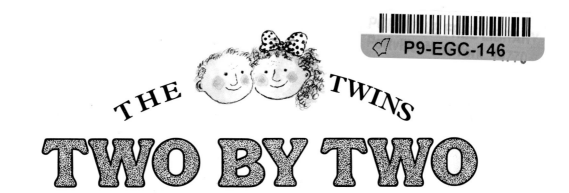

TWO BY TWO

Catherine and Laurence Anholt

CANDLEWICK PRESS
CAMBRIDGE, MASSACHUSETTS

Minnie and Max were having a bedtime story. It was about Noah's ark and all the animals.

"Now it's off to bed two by two," said Mommy.

On the stairs, the twins were tigers...

and in the bathroom, they splashed like crocodiles.

"You sound like two noisy elephants," said Mommy when she came up.

"We're not elephants.
We're two little monkeys,"
said Minnie.

"You certainly are," said
Mommy, tucking them
into bed.

In the dark, the twins were
two bats flying.

Then they jumped around
like kangaroos.

There was so much noise
that Daddy came up.
But where were the twins?

"We're two little bears,"
said a voice from under
the blankets.

Daddy put one little bear
back in his own bed.

But soon Minnie heard
Max crying.

"There's a lion under my
bed," he sniffed.

Minnie was very brave.
She looked under Max's
bed. It wasn't a lion.

It was Ginger!

The twins curled up together and closed their eyes.

"We're two little mice," they whispered – then fell fast asleep.